Surgery on Sunday

By Kat Harrison

Illustrated by
Shane Crampton

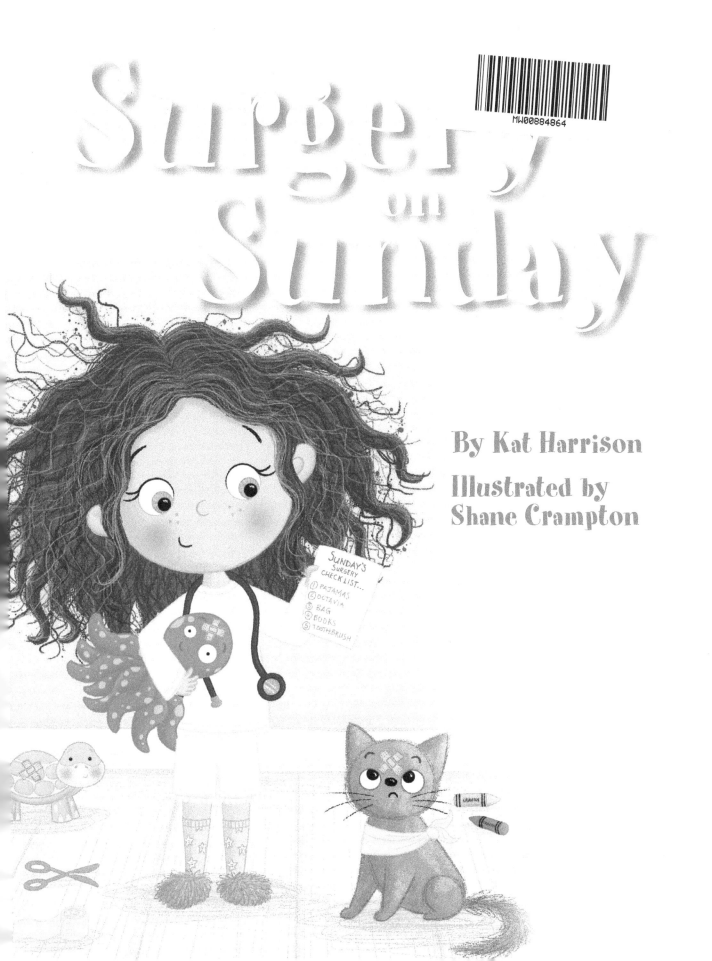

SUNDAY'S
SURGERY
CHECKLIST...
① PAJAMAS
② OCTAVIA
③ BAG
④ BOOKS
⑤ TOOTHBRUSH

ISBN: 978-1-7347075-0-2 (hard cover)
978-1-7347075-1-9 (soft cover)

Editing: Amy Ashby

Published by Warren Publishing
Charlotte, NC
www.warrenpublishing.net
Printed in the United States

To Mom and Dad,
for every waiting room you've sat in–xo, Kat

To Grant, Sam, Finn, and Kai–love, Auntie Shane x

RULE #1

NO EATING OR DRINKING AFTER MIDNIGHT, BOO!

Hi, I'm Sunday. Tomorrow, I am having surgery for the very first time. I'm feeling all kinds of nervous, so I might not sleep more than a miracle minute tonight.

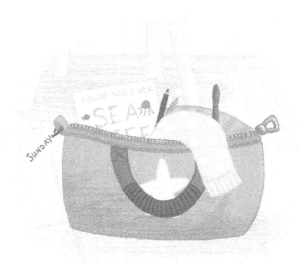

Check!

Hospital bag packed?

My BFF, Octavia the Octopus?

Check! ✓

Check!

Eyes wide open?

Stomach in knots like a triple-tied shoelace?

✓ Check!

In the morning, I arrive at the hospital with my mom and dad. It's so early, the sun is just waking up as the clouds wipe sleep from their puffy eyes. My stomach makes a noise like a monster clearing its throat.

HOSPITAL

ENTRANCE

My parents tell me to wear a brave face, but I'm not so sure what that looks like.

Today, my doctor will fix a tiny tear in my eardrum. "It's as small as a grain of rice," he said at my appointment a few weeks ago. "Patching it up will make you hear better. Think of it like fixing a hole in your jeans."

When we first walk in, the hospital smells
like a cafeteria that's just been wiped down.

"This bracelet is the hospital's way of
making sure you don't get lost."

WAITING
ROOM

Next, a nurse makes me change into a worn-down gown and gray, grippy socks.

"Not even the grown-ups get to wear real clothes in the operating room," she says.

RULE #2
THE HOSPITAL GOWN MAY NOT HAVE A BACK, BUT YOU GET TO KEEP THE SOCKS!

Now it's time to start my IV.
"This is where we will put the medicine that helps you sleep. The medicine will go into your body through a tiny tube in your hand."

Gulp. The needle looks scary, but my dad throws me a thumbs-up and I take a deep breath.

"Can you make a fist for me?" the nurse asks.
I tuck my fingers in and then stretch them out. Tuck
and stretch. She tip-taps my hand like a drum. I picture
my veins popping out like fire-breathing dragons.

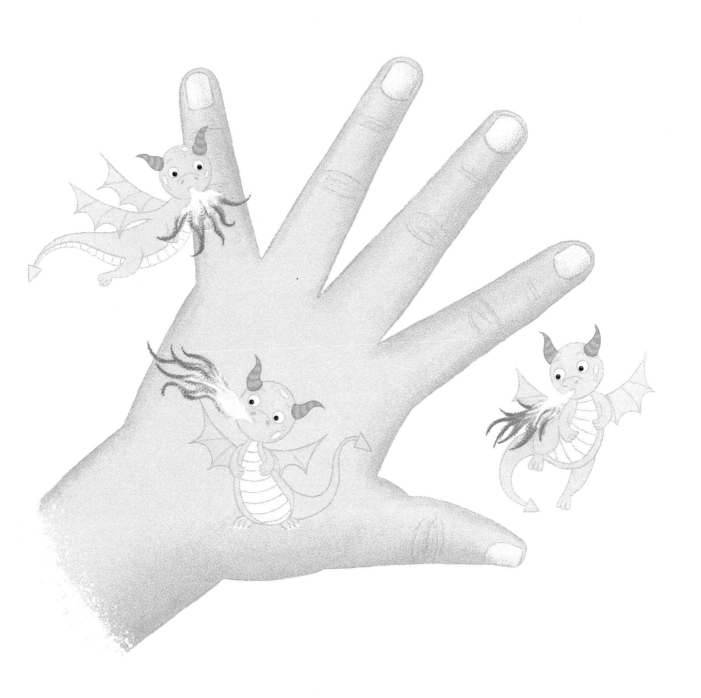

"I can't find a good one,"
the nurse says.

I scrunch my eyes and hold
my breath and wonder
what makes a vein "good."

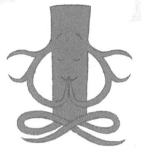

She runs my arm under warm water and wraps me in a hot towel to help my veins come out of hiding. I feel like a mummy and my stomach does a cannonball.

RULE #3
A PEP TALK
GOES A LONG
WAY.

"You can do it, little guys!"

The nurse slips the needle under my skin with a quick pinch and a little poke.

It's not so bad. There is only a little bit of blood and I feel brave.

The doctor visits my bed-on-wheels before surgery. He makes a purple "X" on my right ear with a marker.

"I don't want to forget which side of you we're healing!"

Whenever I'm anxious, my mom tells me to dream of faraway places—like the tippy tops of giant jungle trees and the rocky bottoms of blue-green oceans. Today, I imagine dry dunes of desert sand.

Another nurse arrives to push my bed into surgery.
"I love you, Mom. I love you, Dad."

We all high five as my bed gets rolled down the hallway.
"We'll see you when you wake up, Sunny!" says Dad.
"We'll be in the waiting room the entire time," says Mom.

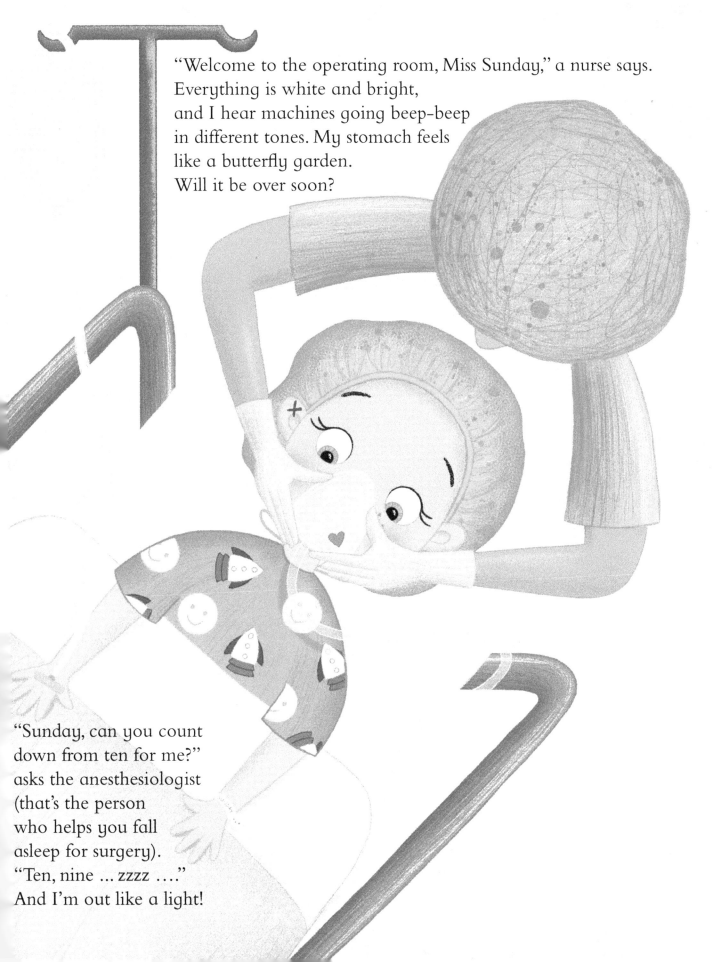

"Welcome to the operating room, Miss Sunday," a nurse says.
Everything is white and bright,
and I hear machines going beep-beep
in different tones. My stomach feels
like a butterfly garden.
Will it be over soon?

"Sunday, can you count
down from ten for me?"
asks the anesthesiologist
(that's the person
who helps you fall
asleep for surgery).
"Ten, nine … zzzz …."
And I'm out like a light!

When I wake up, all I see are blurry faces.
"Would you like ice chips or juice?" asks the nurse.
I choose ice chips because I like the cold against
my tongue. I don't feel like myself today.

I only spend one night recovering in the hospital, but it's tricky to sleep all squished and squashed in the bed like a rollie pollie. I watch a movie to make the time tick by.

NAME: SUNDAY
NURSE: DEBBIE/MANDY
ROOM: 205

PAIN MEASUREMENT SCALE

RULE #4

BRING SOMETHING TO KEEP YOU BUSY.

zzZ

The day after surgery, I get to go home. I feel like
someone filled my body with wet sand—even my eyelids
feel heavy. But neighbors cook homemade spaghetti and
friends bring posters with funny jokes and doodles of
sky-high ice cream "Sundays" to cheer me up.

At my next appointment, the doctor says
the hole in my eardrum has healed.

And in a couple of weeks, I start to feel like
myself again! I can even hear the rumble-
tumble of trains and the chit-chat of cicadas.

RULE #5
YOU'LL GET THROUGH THIS!

Now I know what it looks like to be brave.
Brave looks a little bit like me.

Sunday's (Unofficial) Rules of Surgery

#1 NO EATING OR DRINKING AFTER MIDNIGHT ON THE NIGHT BEFORE SURGERY. BOO!

#2 SHHH, HERE'S A SECRET—THE HOSPITAL GOWN MAY NOT HAVE A BACK, SO YOUR BOTTOM MIGHT GET CHILLY. BUT, AS A BONUS, YOU GET TO KEEP THE SOCKS!

#3 A PEP TALK GOES A LONG WAY, EVEN FOR YOUR VEINS.

#4 IF YOU HAVE TO SPEND THE NIGHT AT THE HOSPITAL, BRING SOMETHING TO KEEP YOU BUSY.

#5 YOU'LL GET THROUGH THIS. LOOK IN THE MIRROR, YOU ARE _SO_ BRAVE!

Let's Talk
Questions to Ask Someone (or Yourself!) Before Surgery

#1
HOW DO YOU FEEL ABOUT HAVING SURGERY? DO YOU FEEL SCARED? EXCITED? CONFUSED? ANGRY?

#2
WHICH PARTS ARE YOU THINKING ABOUT THE MOST?

#3
WHAT'S SOMETHING YOU CAN LOOK FORWARD TO WHEN IT'S DONE? IF YOU GET NERVOUS, TALK TO A GROWN-UP ABOUT THAT SPECIAL THING— LIKE A TREAT, TOY, OR TIME TOGETHER.

#6
WHAT DO YOU EXPECT AFTER SURGERY? IT'S OKAY TO THINK ABOUT HOW YOU MIGHT FEEL OR WHAT YOU'LL DO.

P.S. SURGERY CAN BE TOUGH ON EVERYONE. TAKE CARE OF YOURSELF AND ASK FOR HELP WHEN YOU NEED IT.

#4
WHAT WOULD YOU LIKE TO BRING TO THE HOSPITAL? ASK A FAMILY MEMBER TO HELP YOU PACK!

#5
WHO WILL COME WITH YOU TO THE HOSPITAL? YOU WON'T HAVE TO GO THROUGH THIS ALONE.

CPSIA information can be obtained
at www.ICGtesting.com
Printed in the USA
BVHW022329140521
607150BV00001B/8

9 781734 707519